The chick took another couple of steps until he felt the water against his breast, and very cold it felt too. At that moment he heard the sound of pounding footsteps, and turned to see Jemima – the farmer's daughter – running towards him. Then hands grasped him and scooped him up.

"You silly boy!" said a voice in his ear. "Whatever d'you think you're doing? Anyone would suppose you were trying to swim. Chickens can't, you know. . ."

Can the farmer's daughter find a way to help Frank learn to swim? Find out in this hilarious new story from master storyteller Dick King-Smith.

# DICK KING-SMITH
## Funny Frank

Illustrated by John Eastwood

## YOUNG CORGI BOOKS

FUNNY FRANK
A YOUNG CORGI BOOK : 0 552 55394 8

First published in Great Britain by Doubleday,
an imprint of Random House Children's Books

Doubleday edition published 2001
Young Corgi edition published 2002

Papers used by Random House Children's Books are natural, recyclable products
made from wood grown in sustainable forests. The manufacturing processes
conform to the environmental regulations of the country of origin.

Set in 16/20 pt Bembo Schoolbook

Young Corgi Books are published by Random House Children's Books,
61–63 Uxbridge Road, London W5 5SA,
a division of The Random House Group Ltd,
in Australia by Random House Australia (Pty) Ltd,
20 Alfred Street, Milsons Point, Sydney, NSW 2061, Australia,
in New Zealand by Random House New Zealand Ltd,
18 Poland Road, Glenfield, Auckland 10, New Zealand
and in South Africa by Random House (Pty) Ltd,
Isle of Houghton, Corner of Boundary Road & Carse O'Gowrie,
Houghton 2198, South Africa.

THE RANDOM HOUSE GROUP Limited Reg. No. 954009

A CIP catalogue record for this book is available from the British Library.

Printed and bound in Great Britain by
Cox & Wyman Ltd, Reading, Berkshire.

*Chapter One*

Jemima Tabb was a farmer's daughter.
She was eight years old, she had
dark hair worn in a pigtail, and she
particularly liked chickens, especially
baby chicks.

Whenever one of her father's hens
went broody, Jemima would put a
clutch of eggs under the hen – eggs
that, with luck, would in twenty-one
days' time hatch out into fluffy little
chicks.

Out in the orchard was a duckpond
that was fed by a small stream, and not
far from the edge of this pond was
where Jemima chose to put her broody-

coop with its wire run attached. Sitting
on eggs must be very boring, she thought,
which is why she selected this spot.

"Just you listen to the chuckle of the
water as it falls into the pond, and the
sounds of the ducks quacking and
splashing about, and you'll find the time
will pass quite quickly," she would say
to each broody hen as she settled it
upon the eggs.

Three weeks after she had said all this to a hen called Gertie, eight little chicks duly hatched out.

When the chicks first came out of the coop into the wire run, seven of them scuttled excitedly about on the grass, but the eighth one walked to the end of the run that was nearest to the duckpond

and stood there, quite still, listening to
the chuckle of the water and the sounds
of the ducks quacking and splashing.
From then on, he would do this every
day, standing and gazing and listening,
so that by the time the chicks were a
month old, Gertie – the chick's mother –
was worried and felt she needed to
share her worry.

One fine morning when she and her best friend, Mildred, were scratching about together in the orchard, pecking at worms and beetles and the seeds of flowering grasses, Gertie said to Mildred, "You know, I think that one of my chicks is funny."

"Funny, Gertie?" clucked Mildred. "Do you mean funny (ha! ha!) or funny (peculiar)?"

"Peculiar," replied Gertie. "I've suspected it for some time now. The other seven chicks behave quite normally but this one is different. To begin with, he keeps himself to himself. Look at him now."

Mildred looked at Gertie's chicks as they scuttled about in the grass, pecking at anything and everything, and she saw that there were only seven of them doing this. The eighth chick was standing at the edge of the duckpond, looking at the ducks swimming about in it.

"Is that him?" she asked.
"Yes," replied Gertie.

"Well, he's only looking at the ducks."

"Yes, I know, Mildred. But *why* is he looking at the ducks?"

"Better ask him," said Mildred.

"You!" squawked Gertie at the chick. "Come here!"

At the sound of her voice, the eighth chick turned and came towards them. Usually little chicks run to their mother when she calls them, run very fast, flapping their stubby little wings. But this one was in no hurry.

He came slowly, looking back over his shoulder once or twice at the ducks in the pond, and when he reached the two hens he did not cheep and peep as an ordinary chick would have done. Had Gertie called any one of his brothers and sisters, they would have rushed up to her, saying, "Yes, Mummy?" and probably adding politely, "Good morning, Auntie Mildred."

This chick, though, simply stood there and said, "What?" He did not say it in a rude way, but rather in the tone of someone who has been interrupted in the middle of something important.

"Now," clucked Gertie. "What were you doing?"

"Looking at the ducks," her eighth chick replied.

"Yes, but why were you looking at the ducks?"

"I like ducks," he said. "They're cleverer than you are, Mum."

"Cleverer?" squawked Gertie. "Whatever d'you mean, boy? Compared to hens, ducks are stupid. They can't run about in the grass like we can. They can only waddle."

"Yes," said the chick, "but they can *swim*. I wish I could. It looks nice."

"Don't be silly, dear," his mother said. "Chickens can't swim. Run along now."

This time he did run, straight back to the duckpond, and stood once more at the edge.

Gertie shook her head in amazement. "I told you, Mildred," she said. "That chick is funny."

*Chapter Two*

Gertie and Mildred moved away down the orchard, shaking their heads in a bewildered fashion. On the pond the ducks dabbled happily, while Gertie's eighth little chick watched, wishing and wishing that he could dabble too.

What fun it looked to be playing about in all that lovely water that sparkled in the summer sunshine!

How much they were enjoying ducking their heads under, and letting the glistening stuff slide down their backs, and flapping their wings to spatter themselves with dancing drops, and wagging their rumps with pleasure!

Lucky ducks, he thought. He moved
forward a step or two into the shallows
at the edge of the pond. How cool the
water felt!

Just then a brood of little yellow
ducklings came swimming past.

"Excuse me!" the chick called. "Can I
ask you something?"

The fleet of ducklings turned as one,
and paddled towards him. "Ask away,
chick," they cried.

"Well," he said, "how did you all learn to swim?"

"Learn?" they cried, and they gave a chorus of shrill squeaks that sounded like laughter.

"We didn't learn," one said.

"We didn't have to."

"We just did it."

"Naturally."

"Like ducklings do."

"Well," said the chick, "the thing is — I want to learn to swim."

"Tough luck, chick," they said.

"Chickens can't swim," one added.

"Your feathers aren't waterproof."

"And your feet aren't webbed."

"So, forget it, chick."

"But I can't forget it," said the chick and, in his eagerness to do as the ducklings did, he took another couple of steps forward till the water was up to his knee-joints. "Don't go!" he called to his new friends. "Just tell me, what do I do next?"

And with one voice, they called back one word. "Drown!" And they paddled away making their laughing noises.

The chick took another couple of steps until he felt the water against his breast, and very cold it felt too. At that moment he heard the noise of pounding footsteps, and turned to see Jemima –

the farmer's daughter – running towards
him. Then hands grasped him and
scooped him up.

"You silly boy!" said a voice in his
ear. "Whatever d'you think you're
doing? Anyone would suppose you were
trying to swim. Chickens can't, you
know. Waterproof feathers and webbed
feet – that's what you need for
swimming."

Jemima carried the chick into the kitchen of the farmhouse and was drying his wet bits when her mother came in.

"What have you got there, Jemima?" she asked.

"One of those eight chicks that are out in the orchard, Mum. He was wading into the duckpond, silly boy. Perhaps he thinks he's a duck. I told him, chickens aren't cut out for swimming."

"And what did he say?"

"He made a funny noise, almost as though he was angry at being picked up." She held the chick out before her face. "Didn't you, Frank?"

"Frank? Is that what you are going to call him?" her mother asked.

"Well, that was what the funny noise sounded like. 'Frank! Frank' he squawked. I can't put him back in the orchard, Mum, he'll drown himself, I'm sure he will, won't you, funny Frank?"

"Where are you going to keep him then?"

"I'll put him in that big empty rabbit-hutch till I decide what to do. I'll ask Uncle Ted, he might know."

Uncle Ted was Jemima's father's brother. He was a vet, which was very useful whenever Jemima's father had a sick animal.

Jemima rang her uncle at his surgery.

"Uncle Ted," she said. "It's Jemima. I want to ask you about something. Are you coming anywhere near us today?"

"Yes," said Ted Tabb, "as a matter of fact I am. My last call is only a couple of miles from you. I'll look in if you like. About teatime.

Just in case your mum has got any of those fruit scones about."

"Oh thank you!"

"What's the trouble, Jemima?"

"I've got a chicken that wants to be a duck!"

## Chapter Three

"Tea's ready," called Jemima's mother. "Either of you fancy one of my fruit scones?" she asked, just as her husband and his brother came into the kitchen.

"Yes please, Carrie," said Ted, and "Me, too," said his brother Tom and then, "What's up then, Ted? I never called you."

"No, but Jemima did," said the vet. "Seems she's got a problem with one of her chicks."

"I expect you'll sort it out," said the farmer. "Mind he doesn't charge you too much, Jemima."

When a lot of tea had been drunk and the plate of fruit scones was empty, Jemima's father went off to start the afternoon milking.

"Right," said her uncle. "Let's have a look at this creature of yours."

Jemima went outside and took Frank out of the rabbit-hutch. "He's healthy enough, I think, Uncle Ted, isn't he?" she said.

The vet examined the young chicken. "Looks OK to me," he said, "and you're right – by the look of his comb and the set of his tail, he's a cockerel chick."

"I thought so," said Jemima. "I've called him Frank."

"Well then, Frank," said Ted, "let's go down to the duckpond and see what happens." He went to his car and put on a pair of wellies.

As soon as Frank was put down at the edge of the pond and saw the brood of ducklings come swimming past, squeaking at him, and saw the big ducks dabbling and splashing and preening and heard them quacking happily to each other, he made up his mind.

He would learn to swim. Now! It was now or never. I'll give it a go, he said to himself, and he ran straight into the water.

Once out of his depth, he began to flap his little wings wildly, trying to fly (which he couldn't) and kicked madly with his legs, trying to swim (which he couldn't). Already his feathers were soaked, and now he began to sink until only his head was sticking out. From his gaping beak came one last despairing cry. "Frank!" he squawked.

"Oh, Uncle Ted, he's going to drown!" cried Jemima just as the little fleet of ducklings sailed by, crying, "We told you so!"

"No he isn't," said her uncle, and he waded out into the pond and picked up the waterlogged bird. "Looks like you were right, Jemima," he said. "Frank does want to be a duck, but he's not exactly equipped for it."

"No, I know. He needs waterproof feathers and webbed feet."

"Let's get him dried out," said the vet,
"and stick him back in the rabbit-hutch
and I'll have a good think about you,
funny Frank. In the meantime, don't let
him near that duckpond!"

The very next day Jemima's Uncle Ted
turned up at the farm again. "I've had
an idea," he said. "About Frank."

"What is it?" Jemima asked.

"Well, there can only be one reason
for him going into the duckpond, and
that is that he wants to swim. Now

then, suppose we could help him to do that, make it safe for him to go in the water. He'd be as happy as a pig in muck, Frank would, paddling round with the ducks, wouldn't he now."

"Oh yes!" said Jemima. "But how? I mean, his feathers . . . his feet . . ."

"Tell me this, Jemima," said Ted Tabb. "When people go surfing at the seaside, no matter how cold the sea is, what do they wear?"

"Wetsuits, you mean?" said Jemima.

"Yes," said her uncle. "Go and ask your mum if she's got an old hot water-bottle she could spare . . ."

*Chapter Four*

Frank's mother, Gertie, was extremely worried. She was a very conventional hen who, in her time, had hatched a great many broods of chicks, all of whom had – she liked to think – been properly brought up. That is to say, they were well-mannered and did as they were told and behaved in every way as chicks should.

Now she had somehow managed to produce this funny son, Frank, who was acting in such a very odd fashion. She had seen him with her own eyes walk into the duckpond right up to his knees before the girl had come running to save him.

"Let's hope that will teach him a lesson," she had said to her friend Mildred. "I don't think he'll do that again in a hurry."

But she had been wrong. He had done it again, the same day, and Mildred had seen him do it.

Mildred was by nature a pokenose who liked to stick her beak into everyone else's business. She was also a gossip and she had made sure that the rest of the flock had heard the news before she had run to the bottom of the orchard to tell Gertie about Frank's latest exploit.

"You'll never guess what's happened to Frank!" she panted. "Oh dear, oh dear, it's the end! Poor Gertie, I thought. There was just his little head sticking out of the water, and him calling for help, oh dear, oh dear!"

"He's drowned!" screeched Gertie.
"My little Frank, he's drowned!"

"I don't think so, dear," said Mildred.
"The girl was there with a man who
waded into the pond, rescued your little
lad and took him away. But oh my,
what a worry it must be for you, having
a son like that."

"Like what?" said Gertie.

"Well," said Mildred, "sort of, you
know, not quite . . ."

"Not quite what?" said Gertie rather sharply.

"Well, not quite, er, right in the head," replied Mildred with an embarrassed cackle.

"Mildred," said Gertie slowly and deliberately, "we have been friends for many years, you and I. After your last remark, we are friends no longer." And she stalked off.

The next morning, Gertie was sitting in one of the nest-boxes in the henhouse when Mildred appeared.

"Good morning, Gertie dear," she said.

"It is *not* a good morning," replied Gertie, "and I am about to lay an egg. Kindly go away."

"But I have something important to tell you, dear," said Mildred.

"And I have something important to do, Mildred. Something private and personal. A well-bred hen expects some privacy when she is sitting in her nest-box, for a purpose. I don't wish to do it with someone looking on."

"Oh, sorry, dear," said Mildred. "I'll tell you later on." And she went away.

As soon as she was gone, Gertie raised herself a little and, with a slightly strained expression on her face, laid an egg. She stood up and turned to inspect it. It was, she saw with satisfaction, of a good size and a good colour – a handsome shade of brown. Gertie, something of a snob, rather despised hens that laid white eggs.

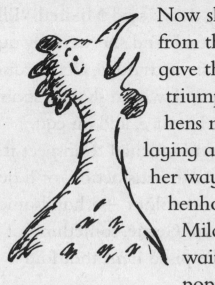

Now she stepped from the nest-box, gave that shout of triumph that all hens make after laying and made her way out of the henhouse.

Mildred was waiting by the pop-hole.

"Well?" said Gertie. "What is this important thing you wish to tell me?"

"It's about Frank, Gertie," said Mildred. "I was having a little look around the place and happened to see him."

"Where?"

"In a rabbit-hutch."

Oh no! thought Gertie. First he wants to be a duck. Now he wants to be a rabbit. "A rabbit-hutch!" she said.

"Poor boy! No room to move about."

"No," said Mildred, "but at least you can't drown in a rabbit-hutch!"

## Chapter Five

Jemima's mother did have an old hot water-bottle that no-one ever used. "But why d'you want it?" she asked Jemima.

"Uncle Ted wants it."

"Whatever for?"

Just then the vet came in.

"Whatever do you want a hot water-bottle for, Ted?" asked his sister-in-law. "Is it to keep a lamb warm?"

"No, Carrie," said

Ted Tabb. "It's to keep a chicken dry. Can I borrow your tape-measure? We must make it fit properly."

"Make what fit?"

"A wetsuit, Mum," said Jemima. "For Frank. So that he can swim."

"Actually we'd be glad of your help, Carrie," said the vet. "I know you're a good dressmaker."

"You're crazy, the pair of you," Jemima's mother said. But to herself she said, if it's worth doing, it's worth doing well.

First they took Frank out of the

rabbit-hutch and made careful notes of his measurements – the length of his back, the breadth of his breast – then they held the hot water-bottle up against him to try for size.

With her dressmaking shears, Jemima's mother cut off the mouth of the bottle and cut right round the edges of it to make two rubber panels. "One for his front, one for his back," she said, "and then I'll stick them together."

"Remembering," said Ted, "to leave a

hole at the end for his head and neck to stick out. Oh yes, and two holes for his legs and another for his tail."

"What about his wings?" Jemima asked.

"Oh yes, and two holes for his wings. He can use those to pull himself along through the water, like an oarsman. It won't matter if they get wet."

"Well I can't guarantee," said Jemima's mother, "that the finished article will be completely waterproof of course, but it should keep most of him pretty dry."

Between the three of them they

managed to hold a protesting Frank and place the two rubber panels against him – front and back – testing for size.

"It'll be miles too big," Jemima said.

"It will now," said her mother, "but don't forget Frank's going to grow. And I'm not making him a whole lot of different-sized wetsuits. This one will have to do."

"Let me know how you get on," said the vet. "I must be off."

Carrie Tabb had never before set out to make a wetsuit for a chicken, but before long Frank was having his first fitting so that she could see exactly where to make the holes for neck, wings, legs and tail. This done, the two panels of the old hot water-bottle were put on Frank, front and back, and then the two halves were stuck together with superglue.

At first Frank protested loudly at the treatment he was receiving, but once the finished wetsuit was finally fitted on him, he seemed to be quite pleased with himself and walked about and flapped his wings and shouted "Frank!" in a loud voice.

That evening, when Tom Tabb had finished milking his cows, he rang up his brother, the vet.

"What time will you finish your surgery, Ted?" he asked.

"About seven, I hope."

"Well, come on over then. Carrie has made this suit for Jemima's chicken and they're going to try it out."

"On the duck-pond?"

"Yes. Seeing as it was your crazy idea, you'd better come to the ceremony. You're invited to the launch of Frank."

So, later, the four Tabbs stood at the edge of the duckpond, wetsuited Frank in Jemima's arms. Around the pond Frank's brothers and sisters were stand-ing, and Gertie and Mildred, and all the other hens of the flock, and the big cockerel. They knew what was going to happen because gossipy Mildred had told them. On the water the ducks and their ducklings cruised.

Now Jemima, in her wellies, waded out into deeper water and carefully lowered Frank on to the surface and let go of him.

He floated.

Loudly the ducks on the pond quacked in amusement. A chicken that floated – weird!

Around the rim the hens squawked in amazement, and the big cockerel gave a loud crow of surprise while Frank's brothers and sisters scampered up and down in excitement.

"He's swimming!" gasped Gertie to Mildred as she gazed upon her wet-suited son.

"Well, not exactly, dear," replied Mildred. "He's floating, certainly, but he's not going anywhere much. He'd have to have webbed feet for that."

Frank was indeed trying to swim. He bashed on the water with his wings and he kicked about with his legs, but neither method propelled him very far. It was plain that Mildred was right, and the watching Tabbs came to the same conclusion.

"You said he'd pull himself along with his wings like an oarsman," said Jemima to her uncle, "but he can hardly move."

"He's too heavy with all that gear on," said her father, and then farmer and vet said with one voice, "He needs webbed feet."

"Right," said Jemima's mother. "Then it's back to the drawing board!"

## Chapter Six

"We can't just leave him there, floating about," said Jemima.

"Go and get some corn and feed the rest of the flock," said her father.

"Yes," said her uncle. "Frank will come out of the pond quick enough then."

And indeed, once Jemima had scattered some handfuls of corn in the orchard grass and the rest were all pecking away at it, Frank managed slowly to scull his way to the pond's edge until at last his feet touched bottom and he could, very clumsily, run to join the others.

All this time, Jemima had been watching, and now she saw that all the

corn had been eaten, leaving none for
Frank. So she fetched another handful
just for him and kept the rest away
while he ate, scratching at the little
heap of corn with his long toes. Great
for scratching, thought Jemima, great for
running on the grass,
but useless for swim-
ming. How could they
help him?

She watched as Frank
pecked up the last
grain of corn and
then looked up at her
enquiringly, head on
one side.

"You're a bright boy, Frank, aren't
you?" she said. "You look at me as
though you can understand what I'm
saying. I just wish you weren't such a
worry to us, wanting to swim like a
duck. I suppose you're going to go
straight back on the pond now?"

For answer, Frank did. He walked right in till he was out of his depth, and then he floated out towards the ducks.

The ducklings were the first to greet him.

"Hi there, chick!" they cried. "That's a cool suit you're wearing!"

"Actually," said Frank, "it's rather hot in the sunshine, when I'm on land, I mean."

"East, West, water's best," chorused the ducklings and away they swam.

Frank worked his legs madly in an effort to follow his young friends, but his clawed feet simply could not propel him along, and fluttering his wings was little help and very tiring. If only I had feet like a duck, he thought, so that I could thrust with my feet like they do and push the water away behind me and go sailing along instead of just floating.

If only those humans would realize that that's what I need. They were clever enough to make me this wetsuit. Surely they could think of some way to make me webs?

Jemima's mother, Carrie *had* been thinking. How could she design a pair of artificial webbed feet? She racked her

brains for some way to do this, and then
by sheer chance, the answer came to her
as she was cleaning the bathroom later
that evening. She was wearing a pair of
rubber gloves as she filled the wash-
basin and scoured it around. They were
bright yellow, these gloves, and some
combination of thoughts about yellow

gloves and ducks' feet and water gave
her the idea. She could – she *would* –
make a pair of artificial webbed feet out
of the rubber gloves. I'll put something
inside the fingers and thumbs to stiffen

them, she said to herself, to help Frank walk (or waddle, rather) on dry land. Then I'll get a sheet of something solid – plywood, perhaps, no plastic, that'll be lighter – and I'll cut out two pieces the shape of a duck's foot and fix one inside each glove like a sort of inner-sole. Then all we shall have to do is stick Frank's feet inside and tape the cuff of each glove around his legs so that no water can get in, and hey presto! Frank will have webbed feet!

## Chapter Seven

One of Jemima's jobs about the farm was, in the evening, to shut up the hens and the ducks in their respective houses, to keep them safe from foxes. She left her mother working on the artificial webbed feet and went out into the orchard.

Sleepy murmurs from the henhouse told her that the flock had already gone to bed, and automatically she bent to close the pop-hole when she thought, Oh Frank! Is he inside? She opened the door of the henhouse. He wasn't.

She went to the duckhouse, outside which several ducks and the big white drake were still pottering about, preening and gabbling softly to one another.

Jemima hooshed them into the house and looked inside, to see all the ducks and all the ducklings – but no Frank.

Quickly she shut the duckhouse door and ran to the duckpond. There, still floating happily out in the middle, was Frank.

When the ducks had begun to leave the pond and waddle away towards the duckhouse, Frank had been in no hurry to follow. He had become rather hot,

wearing as he was a rubber suit over his plumage, and now floating on the nice cold water as the heat went out of the day and the sun sank was so refreshing.

"You coming, chick?" the ducklings called out as they swam past following their mother. "It's time for beddy-byes."

"I think I'll stay here for a bit," Frank replied. "I'm enjoying it."

"Please yourself," they said. "Let's just hope that someone else doesn't enjoy you."

"Who?" asked Frank.

"Mr Fox!" cried the ducklings, and they scuttered off.

For a while Frank continued to float about on the pond, trying to decide what to do. Surely I'll be safe out in the middle here, he thought. Foxes can't swim. Can they? Just then he heard his name called.

"Frank!" cried Jemima. "Come off the pond, you silly boy."

When he made no move, she found a
long stick and waded in till the water
was near the tops of her wellies and
reached out and managed to hook
Frank with the stick and pull him to
shore. Jemima picked him up and
carried him to the henhouse, but when
she went to open the door, he kicked
and struggled and squawked and
shouted "Frank!" in an angry voice.

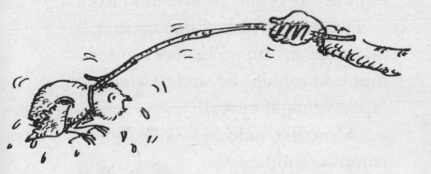

So she took him to the duckhouse. As
soon as she opened its door, he jumped
out of her arms and rushed in.

When she had closed the door,
Jemima listened for a moment. Inside,
the ducks were gabbling quietly and the

ducklings peep-peeping, in a show of welcome, she thought.

In reply her young cockerel said his name several times.

Strange, Jemima thought. It's beginning to sound more like "Quack!" than "Frank!"

"What d'you think of these then, Tom?" said Carrie Tabb to her husband, holding out the results of her handiwork.

The farmer picked one up and inspected it. "By golly, that's a duck's foot and a half," he said. "Grand pair of flippers they'll make."

"More like galoshes really," said Jemima's mother. "Don't forget that Frank has to be able to walk in them as well as swim in them."

"When are you going to fit them on him?"

"Tomorrow morning. Jemima can catch Frank when she lets the hens out."

"No, she can't," said Jemima, coming in. "He wouldn't go to bed with the hens, he's in the duckhouse. Anyway, why must I catch him?"

Her mother and father pointed – one with pride, one with amusement – at the strange pair of artificial webbed feet, bright yellow with five stiffened claws (that had been four fingers and a thumb) and, inside each rubber glove, a piece of stout plastic cut to the shape of a duck's foot.

"Oh, Mum, you are clever!" Jemima said. "I can't wait to see if they work properly."

"Well, wait till I've finished tomorrow morning's milking," said her father. "This is something I don't want to miss."

When, next day, the farmer came into the orchard, his wife and daughter were ready and waiting. They had fitted the new feet to Frank and taped the cuffs of the gloves securely around each leg. He looked a picture, with his brown head and wings and tail poking out of his green hot-water-bottle-wetsuit and his yellow rubber-glove-webs.

Jemima put the young cockerel down on the grass. For a moment Frank stood still, puzzled by the strange things that had been put on his feet. Then he began

to walk, lifting each foot high and
then putting it down again flat on the

ground, rather like a man in snowshoes.
He tripped himself up once or twice due
to the size of his new webs, but then he
got more used to them and began to
make his way towards the duckpond.
He sploshed in the shallows and walked
on in till he was floating.

Jemima held her mother's hand
tightly. "Oh, Mum, it will work, won't
it?" she said.

"Fingers crossed," said her mother,

and they all three crossed them.

Then, as they watched, Frank began to make strong thrusts with his long legs, just the movements he would have made to run on dry land, and immediately he began to move forward, slowly at first, then faster, faster, till he was

swimming around the pond at a speed no duck could hope to match. All the other ducks in fact got hastily out of the way lest they be rammed by this speed-ing water-bird.

"Wow!" the ducklings cried as he whizzed by. "What a swimmer!"

Farmer Tabb summed up the general amazement. "Cor lumme, luvaduck!" he said.

## Chapter Eight

Gertie and Mildred had gone back into the henhouse to lay their day's eggs, and so knew nothing of Frank in all his finery.

They were sitting in adjoining nest-boxes, and Mildred — mindful of the rebuke she had recently received for speaking while Gertie was laying —

kept her beak shut.

Once Mildred
had performed
and gone out,
Gertie laid her
egg and then had
a look at Mildred's
in the next box. It was,

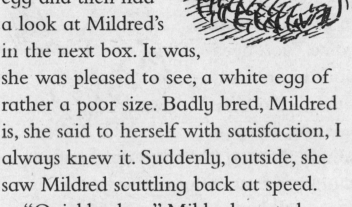

she was pleased to see, a white egg of
rather a poor size. Badly bred, Mildred
is, she said to herself with satisfaction, I
always knew it. Suddenly, outside, she
saw Mildred scuttling back at speed.

"Quickly, dear," Mildred panted.
"Come and have a look at your
Frank!"

"I want nothing more to do with the
boy," said Gertie. "He's nothing but an
embarrassment to me."

"But you must come and look," said
Mildred. "He's really swimming!"

Curiosity is a strong instinct, and
Gertie could not resist making her way

to the duckpond. At the farthest side of it, she saw, was her son, sitting upon the water, quite still.

"If you call that swimming, my dear Mildred," said Gertie in a very sarcastic voice, "you need your brains examining – if you've got any. Frank is simply floating as he has done before, thanks to that awful rubber suit."

Frank was in fact getting his breath back after a great number of high-speed circuits of the pond, but when he saw his mother on the opposite side, he shouted, "Mum! Watch this!" and set off towards her as fast as his webs could drive him. Which was very fast. Up out of the water he surged and stood proudly before his mother in his wetsuit and new yellow footwear.

"What d'you think, Mum?" he said.

For answer, Gertie gave a loud squawk of horror and ran hastily away. What had her son done now! Mildred ran away too, eager to tell the rest of the flock about this latest development.

Frank turned sadly back towards the pond. Over its surface there still ran the waves caused by his recent rapid dash, and on them the ducklings bobbed.

"Wow!" they cried. "You're the greatest!"

"Greatest what?" asked Frank.

"Why, swimmer of course," they said. "Fan-tastic!"

Frank felt a glow of warmth. His mother didn't want to have anything to do with him, nor did his brothers and sisters, nor the big cockerel, nor any of the hens in the flock. But these little ducklings — they were his friends.

"I really *can* swim now, can't I?" he said.

"And how!" cried the ducklings.

"Can I come for a swim with you all now?" Frank asked.

The ducklings looked at each other.

"OK," one said.

"On one condition," said another.

"What?" said Frank.

"Take it a bit slow, chick."

"There's no hurry."

"Nice and easy does it."

"You may like the high-speed stuff . . ."

". . . but we don't."

"Oh, I see what you mean," Frank said. "If I'm dashing about, it makes the water rough so it's not so nice for you. Is that it?"

"You got it," they all said. "It's enough to make us pondsick."

So Frank launched himself back into the water very carefully, and began to swim gently around the duckpond with slow measured thrusts of his big yellow webbed feet and the little yellow ducklings swam with him, like a flotilla of small boats escorting a big ship.

Then the big white drake and all the other ducks, seeing how the ducklings were enjoying the company of the strange chicken, came out on to the water and swam along too, so that Frank found himself at the head of a great armada of ducks.

At last, he thought happily, I am in my element!

## Chapter Nine

It so happened that later that day one
of Tom Tabb's best cows was having dif-
ficulty in calving and so he sent for his
brother the vet. Later, when the calf had
been safely delivered – a heifer calf at
that, which pleased the farmer – Ted
Tabb asked how Jemima's Frank was
getting on.

'You'll be amazed," Tom said. "Carrie has made him artificial feet. I'll just go and get a bowl of corn and we'll go down to the duckpond and you'll see."

By chance all the ducks and the ducklings too were pottering about in the orchard grass, so that the pond was empty of birds except for Frank.

He had been trying to copy his friends who were so good at putting their heads below the surface to pull up weeds or snap up wiggly things. If I'm going to be a proper duck, he told himself, I've got to be able to do that, and so he had been practising. But somehow he didn't seem to have the knack of it.

He could put his
head under all
right (though not
very far – the
wetsuit would not
allow it), but he

wasn't too clever at holding his breath
or keeping his beak closed so that the
water got up his nostrils and down his
throat. Altogether he was fed up and
glad to see the two men approaching,
one holding a bowl of corn and calling
him by name.

Frank went into overdrive. He whizzed across the surface of the pond so fast
that he shot out of
the water onto
the bank,
landing
flat-footed
on his big
yellow
webs.

"What d'you think of that?" asked the farmer.

"Amazing!" said the vet. "Look at those feet! What a rate he goes! Carrie's a genius. But Tom, what's to become of this funny bird that is a chicken but wants to be a duck?"

"Blessed if I know, Ted," said his brother. "I hope he doesn't come to any harm, Jemima's that proud of him. We'll just have to wait and see."

So they waited, as the weeks and indeed the months went by, and they saw Frank grow and grow till he was almost the size of his father, the big red rooster. (Or rather, as big as his father had *been*, for one day, down at the far end of the orchard, he had met an old dog fox that had hidden itself in a nettlepatch.) On

Frank's head now was a big floppy scarlet comb, while out of the back of the wetsuit there hung a fine plumy tail. His wings too had grown enormously so that now he could really scull with them to make his speedy progress on water even speedier. All this time Frank spent his nights in the duckhouse and his days on the duckpond, only coming ashore for food. Of his mother he saw practically nothing, for she kept well away from him, as indeed did his brothers and sisters and the rest of the flock. Sometimes this made Frank feel a little sad, for he was after all a chicken at heart. He had his friends, the ducks, but the older he got the more he began

to realize that though he could swim
like a duck – far better, in fact – he
could never look like one.

He would see his three brothers come
strutting by and think how handsome
they had grown with their fine feathers
and their elegant sharp-clawed feet, in
contrast to his clumsy green rubber suit
and his awkward yellow rubber webs.

A little later he noticed that there
were only two of his brothers, and
later still only one, and at last none.
Where had they gone? Frank wondered.
Little did he dream that they had made

three plump Sunday dinners for the
Tabb family.

For a long time Frank had tried hard,
too, to copy the sounds that all the
ducks made – his first friends, the ducklings, were grown up now – but his
"Quack!" was really still only "Frank!"
But then, one fine morning, something
quite unexpected happened to funny
Frank . . .

Jemima had let the hens out, and
then had opened the duckhouse door,
and all the ducks and the big white
drake and Frank came out and made
for the pond as usual.

The waterfowl went straight onto the

water but Frank, instead of following, jumped clumsily up on top of a big log that lay by the pond's edge. He stood up on his toes (as best he could on his artificial feet, which was not very well), puffed out his chest (though this action, within the wetsuit, could not be seen) stretched out his (by now, very long) neck and, to the astonish- ment of the ducks, gave a loud piercing "Cock-a-doodle-doo!"

*Chapter Ten*

"He crowed, did he?" said Jemima's
father when she told him.

"Yes," said Jemima. "That means he's
a proper grown-up cockerel now, doesn't
it Dad?"

The farmer looked thoughtful. "You
know, Jemima," he said,
"I think it's time you
thought this business
through – I mean,
about Frank wanting
to be a duck. OK,
he enjoys swim-
ming in the pond,

but it's not natural. He should be running around with the rest of the flock, stretching his legs, preening his feathers, behaving like the chicken he is. He can't do any of that while he's dressed up in bits of an old hot water-bottle and a pair of rubber gloves."

"Well what d'you think I should do, Dad?" asked Jemima.

"Nothing for the present. But I think we've got to give him something to tempt him out, something that will be more attractive to him than the ducks."

"Like what?"

"Well," said Jemima's father, "now that he's a big boy, what he needs is a nice girlfriend. That'd really give him something to crow about. Tell you what, next market day, I'll have a look round the poultry pens and see if I can find a pretty little pullet for your Frank."

Frank, too, was thinking of his future. As he watched the flock running helter-skelter across the orchard when Jemima came with food, as he saw them

scratching about in the grass or taking a dust-bath and then preening their feathers, he began increasingly to feel that he had become a prisoner of his own ambition. Because he had wanted to swim like a duck, was he to spend the rest of his life stuck inside his wetsuit so that he couldn't preen or have a dust-bath, with his feet confined in his artificial webs so that he couldn't scratch and couldn't run? He remembered how his late father, the big red rooster, had strutted noisily and proudly amongst his many brown wives. Was he, Frank, never to have a wife of his own?

Over the next couple of days he found himself spending less time on the water and more on the land. At feeding times, he even tried talking to some of the flock, and went as far as saying, "Hello, Mum, how are you?" to Gertie, but she did not answer.

Jemima, meanwhile, was consulting her mother. She it was, after all, who had been to all the trouble of designing Frank's swimming-costume.

"What d'you think, Mum?" she said. "Should we take it off him? He doesn't seem to want to swim as much as he used to."

"If we take it off him, he won't be able to, will he?"

"Can't we just try and see what happens?"

"OK, we'll do it tomorrow. I'm a bit busy today."

*

As things turned out, it was just as well that Jemima's mum postponed the undressing of Frank. For that evening, the old dog fox sneaked back and lay up once more in the nettlepatch. Most of the flock had already made their way up to the henhouse and only Gertie and Mildred were still down at the far end of the orchard, having a last forage in the grass.

Though they were not as firm friends as they had once been, Mildred had partly wormed her way back into Gertie's good books, mostly by toadying to her. Now, looking up at the sky, she said, "Don't you think it's getting late, dear? Time for bed. Come along now."

Gertie did not like to be told. "I'll come when I'm good and ready," she said.

Frank was still standing by the edge of the duckpond. The ducks had gone in, but he stayed, his eye on his distant mother. I'll try and have a word with her as she goes by, he thought. She might give me some advice on what to do.

As he peered down the darkening orchard, he saw the figure of Mildred approaching.

"Isn't Mum coming?" he asked her.

"Don't know, I'm sure," said Mildred huffily as she went by.

I'd better go down and see what she's doing, thought Frank. It'll be dark soon. But then he saw his mother turn and begin to walk up the orchard towards him.

Then he saw a bushy-tailed red shape emerge from the nettlepatch and follow . . .

## Chapter Eleven

"Mum!" yelled Frank at the top of his voice. "Behind you! Look behind you!" and Gertie, doing as she was told for once, came scuttling towards him, wings flapping madly, squawking in panic.

Chickens have always run away from foxes, and Frank should now have fled too. For a moment he was paralysed with fear, knowing that he'd be too slow to escape. But then, unable to bear the sight of his terror-stricken old mother, he set off bravely straight towards the oncoming fox.

"Keep going, Mum!" he cried as Gertie dashed past, and then he marched on towards the old enemy, lifting his great yellow webs high and stamping them down again while loudly crying "Frank! Frank!"

The fox stopped in his tracks. What kind of chicken was this that was coming directly at him, shouting some kind of war-cry? What kind of chicken was this that wore a coat of green armour, that had huge webbed feet, and smelt strongly of duck-pond? The old dog fox's nerve broke, 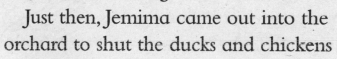 and he turned tail and slunk away.

Just then, Jemima came out into the orchard to shut the ducks and chickens up for the night. She heard her cockerel's cries and ran, just in time to see the worsting of the fox. "Oh Frank, Frank!" she called, and then she hurried to pick him up.

"What a brave boy you are!" she said as she carried him to the duckhouse. But when she came to its door, he kicked and struggled and squawked and shouted his name in an angry voice. So she took him to the henhouse, and he jumped out of her arms and dashed in.

On one of the perches, a breathless Gertie had been telling Mildred what had happened.

"There was a fox . . ." she panted.

"I told you, didn't I?" said Mildred. "I told you it was getting late."

"Oh be quiet and listen," said Gertie, "because if it hadn't been for Frank, you would never have heard my voice again."

"Oh dear, oh dear," said Mildred.

"He saved my life!" said Gertie. "He charged at that fox so that I could have time to escape. I only hope he died quickly. Oh my brave Frank, he gave his life for mine." She closed her eyes and sat in silent mourning.

"I don't think he did, dear," said Mildred, for at that moment Frank came dashing in through the henhouse-door which Jemima closed behind him.

Gertie opened her eyes to see, standing in the gloom, the rubber-clad figure of her son. "It's a ghost!" she murmured to Mildred in horror.

"I don't think it is, dear," said Mildred.

"I'm not a ghost, Mum," said Frank. "I'm solid flesh and blood."

"And rubber," said Mildred.

"Yes, I think that's what scared that old fox. He'd never seen a cockerel like me."

"There's never *been* a cockerel like you, my boy!" cried Gertie. "You saved Mummy's life, you're a hero!"

Frank looked down his beak modestly.

"And it's lovely to have you back here with us instead of being with those old ducks," said Gertie. I daresay it was his funny gear that frightened that fox, she thought drowsily as she drifted towards sleep. But I wish he'd get rid of it . . .

*Chapter Twelve*

The very next day Jemima's father
went to market and found just what
he'd been looking for.

"Come and see what I've got for
you," he said to his daughter when he
arrived home. He took a crate out of
the back of the Land-Rover.

"Oh, Dad!" cried
Jemima. "Is it a girl-
friend for Frank?"

"Yes. What d'you
think of her?"

Jemima lifted out
of the crate a pullet

of a particularly pretty colour. She was
not brown like all the other hens in the
flock. She was speckled, her white
feathers covered in little black dots.

"She's gorgeous!" cried Jemima softly.
"Shall I take her out and introduce her
to Frank?"

"I think I'd leave it till
the morning," said
Tom Tabb. "It's get-
ting late, it'll be
dark soon. Stick her
in the old rabbit-
hutch for tonight
with some food
and water and
we'll put her out tomorrow."

"Tomorrow," Jemima said, "Mum's
going to take Frank's wetsuit and webs
off."

"Wait till she has, then. This little girl
might get a bit of a shock if she meets
Frank in all his funny gear."

She won't get a shock, thought Jemima as she lay in bed that night. She'll probably think he looks really cool.

So next morning, when she went to let the flock out, she caught up Frank and carried him to the rabbit-hutch. Frank looked in, to see a vision of speckled beauty. He let out a strangled croak. It was love at first sight!

The pullet's reaction at seeing him was rather different. She put her head on one side and regarded him with a bright eye.

"Coo-er!" she said. "You don't half look funny."

"Funny (ha! ha!) or funny (peculiar)?" asked Frank.

"Both," replied the pullet and she turned her back on him.

Frank looked crestfallen.

"Don't worry," Jemima said to him. "Wait till we get all that old stuff off you." With the help of her mother, she unstuck the wetsuit and took off the artificial webs, then Jemima took Frank out into the orchard and let him go.

Hope he doesn't try to swim now, she thought, ready to rescue him if he should. But grown-up Frank seemed to have more sense. To be sure, he waded a little way into the pond on his long legs to say good morning to his web-footed friends, but no further. Then he ran lightly off and began to scratch about in the grass with those sharp claws he'd never properly used, and gave himself a good dust-bath, and shook his bright-red feathers, hidden for so long under their rubber covering, and began thoroughly to preen himself. Then he jumped easily onto the top of the big log and stood up on his toes and puffed out his chest and stretched out his neck and crowed a loud triumphant crow.

Gertie had just re-entered the hen-house to lay an egg when Mildred came dashing in.

"Quickly, come quickly, dear!" she screeched.

"I have told you before, Mildred . . ." began Gertie, but Mildred continued, unabashed.

"It's Frank!" she cried. "You'll never guess!" and she rushed out again.

Frank, from having been the bane of Gertie's life, was now – thanks to his saving of that life – the apple of her eye, and she forgot both her cry of triumph at laying and her dignity and went tearing after her friend.

"Where is he? What's happened? Is he all right?" she cried, and then she saw, standing upon the log by the pond, a magnificent young red cockerel. Who's he? she thought. "Where's my Frank?" she said.

"There, dear," said Mildred. "On the log. That's him. They've taken his clothes off. Isn't he handsome!" And as she

spoke, Frank gave another
loud triumphant crow.

At that moment Jemima
came out carrying
the speckled pullet
and put her down
on the grass and
watched her scamper
towards the new
Frank and stop by
the log to gaze up at
him.

"Hello," said the pullet. "Where have
you been all my life?"

Inside a wetsuit, thought Frank. "I
think we've met before," he gulped.

"We certainly have not," replied the
speckled pullet. "The only guy I've met
since I arrived last evening was a weird-
looking wally dressed up as a duck.
As different from you as could be. Hope
I don't meet him again."

"You won't," said Frank. "He's gone.

By the way, my name's Frank. What's yours?"

"Haven't really got a name," she said. "My mum just called us all 'chick'."

Frank hopped off the log and stood beside her. "I'd call you gorgeous," he murmured softly.

"I like it!" cried the speckled pullet. "Sounds nice. You're Frank, I'm Gorgeous."

"Oh, my!" said Mildred from where she and Gertie were standing. "How I should love to know what they're saying!"

Normally Gertie would have replied to such a remark with a cutting answer such as "The world would be a better place if

everybody minded their own business."
But now she stood in a kind of daze,
staring at her handsome hero of a son
and the new arrival. She looks to be
well-bred, she thought, and that speckled
colour is so distinguished. I bet she will
lay the brownest of eggs. Then she saw
the pullet run off down the orchard,
pursued by her boy.

"Don't they make a lovely couple,
dear!" said Mildred. "You'll be having
more pretty grandchildren one of these
fine days."

"Mildred," said Gertie dreamily. "For
once, you're right."

The rest of the flock had been staring

too, first at the new-look Frank and then at the very pretty pullet. The ducks, too, watched proceedings with much interested quacking.

"We miss Frank," those ducks that had once been his little duckling friends said to their father, the big white drake. "D'you think he'll ever come swimming with us again, Dad?"

"He will not," said the drake. "He's a nice boy, Frank is, but it wasn't wise of him to try and be a duck. Ducks are cleverer than chickens, you see. We can walk about *and* we can swim. Chickens can only walk about. They can't swim."

★

That afternoon Carrie Tabb tempted her brother-in-law, the vet, to come over to tea (she'd just made a fresh batch of fruit scones), and so the four of them – Tom and Carrie, Jemima and her Uncle Ted – leaned on the orchard gate and watched as Frank strutted proudly past, Gorgeous at his side.

"Funny, Frank, wasn't he?" said Jemima.

"How d'you mean?" they said.

"Well, wanting so much to be a duck. He doesn't any more, does he?"

"He's found his true place," they said.

"And his true love!" said Jemima, and they all smiled happily.

Frank and Gorgeous stood wing-tip to wing-tip by the edge of the duck-pond. Frank's friends swam by, loudly quacking his name in greeting.

"Stupid creatures!" said Gorgeous, tossing her pretty head. "Sploshing about in that stuff. Why, water's only for drinking, any fool knows that."

"I suppose so," said Frank, "but don't you ever think it would be nice to be able to swim?"

"To swim?" cried Gorgeous. "A chicken, swimming? Oh, Frank, you are funny!"

THE END